Delicious English
CARAMEL TREE

www.carameltree.com

The TurkeyS Who Learned to Speak Moo

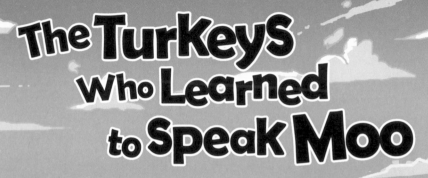

CARAMEL TREE

Chapter 1

'GLUGLUGGLUGLUGLUG'

All the turkeys in Farmland were ordinary turkeys. They were not unusual turkeys. They were just plain ordinary turkeys. But they were busy turkeys. They were busy pecking at the grains on the floor. They were busy trying not to eat things they shouldn't. And of course, they were busy speaking Gobble like this:

"GLUGGLUGLUGLUGGLUG," which means 'Gobble gobble. Gobble gobble gobble.'

The turkeys gobbled all the same, and they gobbled loud. With so many turkeys all gobbling at once, it was very noisy in the turkey pen.

GLUGLUGG
GLUGLUGG
GLUGLUGG
GLUGLUGG
GLUGLUGG
GLUGLUGG
FL 2651

At Farmer Bolton's farm, the turkeys were much the same as the turkeys from all over Farmland. But there was one turkey, called Samson, who was not an ordinary turkey. He was really quite extraordinary.

He was smart and watchful. He liked watching the other turkeys waddle this way and that, pecking at one thing or another. Samson watched carefully, looking for little dangers and stopping small accidents.

Samson's watchful nature also meant that he got to know the other turkeys. He knew that André was always the first to get up, and that Zane always came last. He knew that Bill was always bumping into things, and Pete was always pooping. He knew that Shawn was the loudest gobbler, and Luke never looked at what he was eating.

"Look out, Luke!" shouted Samson. "You don't want to eat that. That's Pete's poop!" If only Luke could hear him.

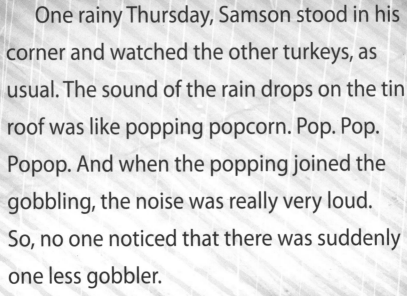

One rainy Thursday, Samson stood in his corner and watched the other turkeys, as usual. The sound of the rain drops on the tin roof was like popping popcorn. Pop. Pop. Popop. And when the popping joined the gobbling, the noise was really very loud. So, no one noticed that there was suddenly one less gobbler.

The turkeys gobbled as usual. But Samson listened to the noise and noticed something different. He could not hear Shawn, the loudest gobbler of them all. Samson decided to look around more closely. He noticed that some of the other turkeys were also absent. There were at least three other turkeys missing.

'Where could they be?' Samson worried.

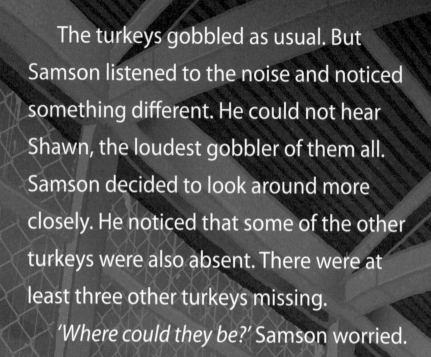

Chapter 2
Samson Is Horrified

The next Thursday, most of the turkeys were up early, gobbling away as they ate the fresh grain Farmer Bolton had brought. Samson watched Farmer Bolton sprinkling the grain. Samson could not eat. He was worried about Shawn and the other three turkeys. He looked over to count everyone again and couldn't see Zane.

'Oh no!' thought Samson, 'not Zane also!' But then he remembered that Zane was always the last to wake up. Samson smiled in relief as he saw Zane waddle down into the pen.

But then, Samson saw something horrific while all the other turkeys' heads were down. He saw Farmer Bolton grabbing Zane and taking him away. Zane flapped his wings desperately, but the farmer's grip was tight.

Samson was horrified. He watched helplessly as Zane disappeared into the farmer's truck.

As the truck drove away, Samson knew Zane would not be coming back. Samson knew that Shawn and the other three turkeys would also not be coming back. They had been taken away forever.

Chapter 3
Samson Has a Plan

Samson looked around the pen and saw the other turkeys happily pecking at the fresh grain. But Samson could not eat. He knew that Farmer Bolton would come back and take each one of them away forever. Samson had to warn the other turkeys.

Better still, he had to come up with a plan to stop any more of the turkeys from being taken away. And, being a watchful turkey, Samson soon came up with a plan.

That afternoon, Samson called a meeting. It was difficult to get all the turkeys' attention. But he finally managed by shouting, "Watch out! The roof is falling down!" All the turkeys looked up. There was a moment of silence, and that was enough for Samson to tell the other turkeys the awful truth. Farmer Bolton was going to take them away one by one, and they would never come back.

The other turkeys listened in horror.

"What can we do?" asked André.

"How can we stop this?" asked Pete.

"Easy!" said Samson. "We must learn to speak Moo."

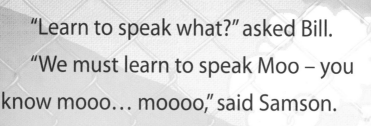

"Learn to speak what?" asked Bill.

"We must learn to speak Moo – you know mooo… moooo," said Samson.

"What do you mean?" asked André.

"Look," pointed Samson. "The cows speak Moo, and they get such special treatment. Farmer Bolton comes and massages them every day. They get washed and can stroll around freely in the fields. But we speak Gobble, and we are stuck inside this pen."

"Yes," said André. "If we learn to speak Moo, we can be just like the cows. Free!"

"We'll get massages?" Pete smiled at the thought.

"We'll be able to have a bath," added Bill.

"Yes, yes, yes," said Samson. "And none of us will disappear again."

So the turkeys listened carefully to the cows' voices.

'Moo'

'Moooo'

'Moo'

'Mo'

'Moooo'

It wasn't difficult to learn to speak Moo.

Chapter 4
Famous

The next Thursday, when Farmer Bolton came to the pen, he was surprised to hear all the mooing.

The farmer looked at the turkeys and said, "What's going on? This is amazing. I am going to be rich!"

He called the local newspaper, which then ran a story on the turkeys. 'Turkeys Learn to Speak Moo' – read the headline.

Soon, there were videos of the mooing turkeys all over the Internet and on every TV station. They became famous.

The turkeys were instant celebrities. They were washed and blow-dried. They were massaged and petted. They even got to leave the pen and run around freely.

The next Thursday, Samson watched as Farmer Bolton brought them the best grain ever and then walked away empty-handed. His plan was working. No more turkeys disappeared.

The news of the mooing turkeys spread across Farmland. Other farmers brought their turkeys to Farmer Bolton's farm. They wanted their turkeys to learn to speak Moo so they could become famous, too.

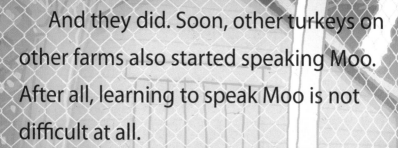

And they did. Soon, other turkeys on other farms also started speaking Moo. After all, learning to speak Moo is not difficult at all.

It wasn't long before mooing turkeys became normal. All the turkeys in Farmland mooed, so they were not news anymore. They were just ordinary turkeys.

Chapter 5
Not Special Anymore

Then Thursday came, and the mooing turkeys became one moo quieter. And on the next Thursday, another mooing turkey went silent.

The turkeys were alarmed.

"He's taking us away again," they cried.

"How can we stop him?"

"We are not special anymore," said André.

"We need to be special again!" shouted Bill.

"Look!" pointed Samson. "The dog gets such special treatment. He gets petted and pampered. We must learn to speak Woof!"

8